W9-CME-239

DATE DUE

DEC 1 7 1998	JUL 2 7 2011		
JUL 2 0 2001			
AUG 2 8 2001	JUN 2 8 2011		
JUL 1 2 2002			
JUL 2 4 2002	OCT 1 9 2011		
JUL 2 7 2004			
JUL 0 4 2006			
AUG 2 1 2008			
NOV 2 0 2008			
JUN 2 7 2009			
JUL 1 5 2010			

Schnitzel von Krumm
Forget-Me-Not

Lynley Dodd

Gareth Stevens Publishing
MILWAUKEE

With pattering paws
and a lolloping tum,
down the front steps
galloped Schnitzel von Krumm.

Out on the drive
by the barbecue bar,
the family loaded
the trailer and car.
In went the tent
and the old red canoe;
paddles
and blankets
and sleeping bags too.
Such a scurrying bustle,
a holiday hum —
it was all of a puzzle
to Schnitzel von Krumm.

He meddled and snooped
from the gate to the shed,
he got under feet
until everyone said,
"We're all in a hurry,
we MUST get away,
so Schnitzel von Krumm —
PLEASE —
keep out of the way!"

7

He scruffed into boxes,
he climbed into bed,
he drove them all mad
until everyone said,
"We're all in a hurry,
we MUST get away,
so Schnitzel von Krumm —
PLEASE —
keep out of the way!"

At last they were ready,
the packing was done,
they gathered the children
and counted each one.
They checked up on Grandma,
the food
and the tent,
they fastened their seat belts
and off they all
went.

Poor Schnitzel von Krumm.
He whimpered and yowled,
he sat by the gate
and he howled
and he howled,
"ow-ow-ow-ow-OW-OW-ow!"

His woebegone misery
bothered Miss Plum.
"NO!" she said, "Surely
that's Schnitzel von Krumm?"

Far out of town
at the side of the road,
the family stopped
and inspected the load.
They started to worry,
"We can't carry on —
something is horribly,
terribly
wrong."

17

"We packed all the children,
the tent and canoe,
the paddles
and blankets
and sleeping bags too.
We tied down the surfboards
and Grandma has come,
but
something is missing —
WHERE'S SCHNITZEL VON KRUMM?"

"Oh doom
and disaster,
what absence of mind;
we just didn't notice —
WE'VE LEFT HIM BEHIND!
Poor little Schnitzel,
alas and alack,
we simply can't help it —
we'll have to go
back."

But
chasing behind
like a hurricane gust,
came a skidding of tires
and a billow of dust.
Catching them up
was speedy Miss Plum
and
WHO was her passenger?

SCHNITZEL VON KRUMM!

What a commotion;
he gamboled around
in a frolicking frenzy,
a rollicking bound.
He capered in circles
till,
breathless at last,
he sank in a heap
at the edge
of the
grass.

27

"COME!"
said the family,
"Let's get away;
that's quite enough drama
and fuss
for today."
They fastened their seat belts
and waved to Miss Plum
as they set off together
with . . .

Schnitzel von Krumm.

For a free color catalog describing Gareth Stevens Publishing's list of high-quality books and multimedia programs, call 1-800-542-2595 (USA) or 1-800-461-9120 (Canada). Gareth Stevens Publishing's Fax: (414) 225-0377. See our catalog, too, on the World Wide Web: http://gsinc.com

GOLD STAR FIRST READERS

A Dragon in a Wagon
The Apple Tree
Find Me a Tiger
Hairy Maclary from Donaldson's Dairy
Hairy Maclary Scattercat
Hairy Maclary, Sit
Hairy Maclary's Bone
Hairy Maclary's Caterwaul Caper
Hairy Maclary's Rumpus at the Vet

Hairy Maclary's Showbusiness
The Minister's Cat ABC
Schnitzel von Krumm Forget-Me-Not
Schnitzel von Krumm's Basketwork
Slinky Malinki
Slinky Malinki, Open the Door
The Smallest Turtle
Wake Up, Bear

Library of Congress Cataloging-in-Publication Data

Dodd, Lynley.
    Schnitzel von Krumm forget-me-not / by Lynley Dodd. — North American ed.
      p. cm. — (Gold star first readers)
    Summary: Schnitzel von Krumm's family is busily packing to go on vacation but, in their eagerness to get on the road, they forget something very important.
    ISBN 0-8368-2094-0 (lib. bdg.)
    [1. Dogs—Fiction. 2. Stories in rhyme.] I. Title. II. Series.
PZ8.3.D637Sb   1998
[E]—dc21
                                      97-35445

North American edition first published in 1998 by
Gareth Stevens Publishing
1555 North RiverCenter Drive, Suite 201
Milwaukee, Wisconsin 53212 USA

First published in 1996 in New Zealand by Mallinson Rendel Publishers Ltd., Wellington, New Zealand. Original © 1996 by Lynley Dodd.

Printed in Mexico

1 2 3 4 5 6 7 8 9 02 01 00 99 98